Emma and Lindsey gave Charlie Miss Claudine's message. "If your foot is better by Wednesday, you can still be in the show," Lindsey told her.

"Oh, I doubt it will be better by then," Charlie insisted. "Darn this stupid TV!" Charlie got up and crossed the room to adjust the color.

Lindsey and Emma looked at one another in surprise. "Doesn't your foot hurt when you do that?" Lindsey asked her.

Charlie was speechless. In her frustration she had forgotten to limp. "Umm . . . the pain comes and goes," she stammered.

"Don't lie to us, Charlie Clark," said Emma indignantly. "You're faking!"

"Shhh!" Charlie hissed, looking around to make sure none of her family was nearby. "It's just until after the show is over."

"You can't do that. It's not fair," said Lindsey. "We have to be in it, so you do, too."

"I do not," Charlie argued. "You're just jealous because I found a way out of it and you haven't."

Emma told Charlie what they had overheard Miss Claudine saying to Adrian about possibly having to close the school. "She counting on us to do a good job on Eastbridge Day so that other kids will sign up and she won't lose her school. We can't let her down."

Charlie felt trapped. She did want to help Miss Claudine. But she did *not* want to be in the show.

What should she do?

Other Books in the **NO WAY BALLET** series:

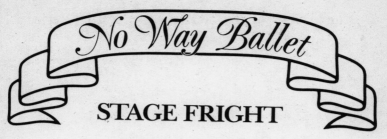

No Way Ballet

STAGE FRIGHT

Suzanne Weyn

Illustrated by Joel Iskowitz

Troll Associates

Library of Congress Cataloging-in-Publication Data

Weyn, Suzanne.
   Stage fright / by Suzanne Weyn; illustrated by Joel Iskowitz.
     p.   cm.—(No way ballet ; #4)
   Summary: Charlie hopes that a sprained ankle will keep her from
having to perform in a ballet recital.
   ISBN 0-8167-1651-X (lib. bdg.)   ISBN 0-8167-1652-8 (pbk.)
   [1. Ballet dancing—Fiction.]   I. Iskowitz, Joel, ill.
II. Title. III. Series: Weyn, Suzanne. No way ballet ; #4.
PZ7.W539Sr 1990
[Fic]—dc19   89-31349

A TROLL BOOK, published by Troll Associates,
Mahwah, NJ 07430

Printed in the United States of America.

10 9 8 7 6 5 4 3 2 1

STAGE FRIGHT

Chapter One

Charlie Clark checked over her shoulder. The boys were still behind them, shoving one another and laughing at who knew what private jokes. Even though it was a cold January day, two boys squirted one another with water pistols, while another two were engrossed in a spitting contest.

"Don't keep looking at them," Emma Guthrie scolded her friend as they walked along a few paces ahead of the boys. "You'd never know they were in the same fifth-grade class as we are. They act more like first-graders."

"There's that stupid Ronnie Small," whispered Lindsey Munson, looking back quickly. "Last year his mother called my father to complain that I'd hurt her little Ronnie when we were playing touch football. What a baby!"

"Stop watching them. It just makes them act weirder," Emma insisted.

Charlie tried to fix her gaze straight ahead. But the

more she concentrated on looking forward, the more difficult it became. It was as if some irresistible force was pulling her head around, making her want to sneak one quick peek. That force had a name: Mark Johnson.

She, Emma, and Lindsey always walked home this way from Eastbridge Elementary. So did lots of kids from the school. The girls usually just ignored the boys, but lately Charlie found herself very aware of Mark; a tall, thin boy with curly black hair and blue eyes. She couldn't really understand why. He'd been in her class ever since the fourth grade and she'd never paid much attention to him before.

Now she was painfully aware of the group of boys getting closer and closer to them. Mark was in the group. That's what made it so hard to walk straight ahead without looking back.

"Hey! Clark!" Charlie turned and saw the boy named Ronnie Small shouting at her. "I didn't know you were such a genius in history."

Charlie felt herself redden with embarrassment. That day she'd given her oral report on the American Revolution. She'd thought she was in good shape, having taken all her information from the mini-series on George Washington she'd been watching on TV that week. Unfortunately, when Charlie reported, "And then George swept Martha into his arms and kissed her. 'Martha,' he said, 'you're the only one for me,'" the class had begun giggling uncontrollably.

She'd assumed everything on the show was historically correct, but soon discovered her mistake. Her teacher, Mrs. Harding, kept shaking her head every

time Charlie talked about the love lives of Paul Revere or Thomas Jefferson. To Charlie, that had been the most interesting part of the series, so she had naturally included it.

"Oh, Martha, Martha, I just adore you," Ronnie taunted now, planting loud, smacking kisses on the back of his hand while the boys behind him laughed. Charlie saw Mark look away, but he was definitely smiling at Ronnie's joke.

"Stop it, George," Ronnie continued in a high-pitched, shrill imitation of a woman's voice. "Your false teeth will come unglued."

"Shut up, Small, or I'll unglue *your* teeth," Lindsey said, leaping to her friend's defense.

"Just try it, Munson," Ronnie snarled back.

"Why? So you can go tell your mother I hurt her itty bitty baby again?" Lindsey teased.

"You're full of it," Ronnie snapped irritably. But apparently he didn't want Lindsey to mention the football story in front of his friends, because he went back to the group of boys and left the girls alone.

Charlie wished she could disappear. It was bad enough that she had to bring home a note from Mrs. Harding saying, "Charlie watches entirely too much TV" and telling all about her report. She'd also humiliated herself in front of the class—and Mark.

Looking at her two friends walking next to her, Charlie realized they were trying to hold back their laughter. "What's so funny?" she demanded.

"Your report," Emma confessed with a giggle. "Did you read anything at all before you wrote it?"

"*The TV Guardian* had an article on the mini-series," Charlie told her stiffly.

"That's what you read?" Lindsey shouted.

Charlie shrugged. "Okay, so it was a dumb report."

"But it *was* the only report that didn't put me to sleep," Emma admitted.

"I know," Charlie agreed. "Everything is more interesting on TV."

They turned down the block toward Charlie's house. Emma and Lindsey waved good-bye as they continued on their way. "See you tomorrow at ballet class," Lindsey called.

"Yeah, see you," Charlie answered as she cut across her lawn. *Lucky me,* she thought sourly. *I'll get a chance to look like a jerk again tomorrow.* No matter how hard she tried, Charlie was the worst dancer in Miss Claudine's School of Ballet. Emma and Lindsey were pretty bad—but Charlie was the worst.

"Anybody home?" Charlie called as she let herself in the front door and hung her jacket in the closet. There was no answer. Good. She would have a few moments alone in front of the TV to help her forget about this disastrous day.

She settled onto the big plaid couch in the living room and used the remote control to click on the TV. "The search for love never ends," a man's deep voice spoke from the set, and Charlie smiled. She'd tuned in just in time. *Search for Love* was her favorite daytime soap. Now the central character, beautiful, dark-haired Reva Harris, was talking to her boyfriend, Lance, on the veranda of her estate. "Lance, Lance,"

5

Reva begged, "you have to believe it wasn't me who said all those terrible things. It was Nina, my twin. She's out of her mind."

Charlie tried to imagine that she was no longer a skinny, red-haired ten-year-old. Instead she was gorgeous Reva, and she was talking to Mark Johnson. "That was my twin Nina in school the other day," she was telling him. "She knocked me out and then gave that terrible report just to make me look bad. She's out of her mind." If only it were that easy.

Mark Johnson. Mark Johnson. Why couldn't she stop thinking about him? There was nothing really remarkable about him—except that he didn't seem quite as dumb as the other fifth-grade boys. There was something quiet and nice in his manner, even though he joked around and teased like the others.

"I'm so confused," Lance spoke from the TV. "I don't know what to believe. If only—" The TV suddenly went dark. Charlie turned and saw her mother holding a basket of laundry under one arm and the remote control in her opposite hand. She'd been so preoccupied that she hadn't even noticed her mom coming in and picking up the remote.

"Hi, Mom." Charlie sat up guiltily, knowing she was forbidden to watch television until after supper. "I didn't know you were home."

"I was in the basement," said her mother, putting down the wash and sitting beside Charlie on the couch. "You know the rule about TV."

"Sorry. But can't we just make an exception for *Search,* please?"

"It didn't look as if you were even paying attention

to it," said her mother, starting to fold clothes as she spoke. "You seemed to be a million miles away."

"I was thinking about stuff," Charlie answered.

"Anything in particular?"

"It's kind of strange, Mom," she began hesitantly. "There's this boy in my class and I just think about him all the time. I don't even know him that well. He says hi to me and all, but we're not good friends. I can't stand it. It's like I want to open up my head and pull out all the thoughts that have to do with him. I hate it."

Mrs. Clark smiled. "I was just about your age when I had my first crush on a boy."

"Crush!" Charlie gasped, horrified. "No, it's not that. I don't even like boys to hang around with, the way Lindsey does. It's more like I have some terrible mental sickness that keeps me stuck on this one subject."

Charlie's mother snapped a T-shirt she'd been folding at her daughter. "The only mental sickness you have comes from being glued to that set all the time. It's natural to start thinking about boys, Charlie. And when you have a crush on someone, you think about him all the time."

"I don't want to have a crush on some boy," said Charlie. "I don't like the way it feels."

"Try thinking about other things," suggested Mrs. Clark.

"Like what?"

Mrs. Clark thought a moment. "Tell me how ballet's going."

"Don't ask," Charlie said with a moan. "We've

been practicing this scene from *Swan Lake,* and we're all supposed to be these magical swans who dance around that snotty girl, Danielle—the one I was telling you about. She's the Swan Princess and she thinks that makes her queen of the world. Anyway, whenever the class is going in one direction, I'm going in the other. If they're up, I'm down. If I'm up, *they're* down. Miss Claudine is nice, but I think she's getting totally fed up with me."

"I'm sure you're not as bad as you think," her mother said.

"Believe me, I'm even worse. Please, let's talk about something else."

Mrs. Clark sat back on the couch. "Okay, how was school?"

"*School?*" Charlie repeated, as if her mother had asked how her trip to Mars had been. "School?" She knew she was stalling. She had to return the note from Mrs. Harding the next day, and it had to be signed by one of her parents. Any discussion of school would inevitably have to lead to the report and the note. There was no sense delaying. The last three times she'd tried to sign her mother's name to something she'd been caught. Forgery just wasn't one of her talents.

"Do you remember the time we talked about how some TV programs can be very educational?" she began, rising and fishing through her school backpack. "And remember you agreed that some shows are really pretty interesting and informative?"

"I remember," said her mother, looking suspicious. "But what does this have to do with school?"

"*Weeellll* . . ." Charlie scrunched up her face and held the note out to her mother. "I gave this report today, and . . . and . . . well, it's all here in this note . . . . "

Chapter Two

"Now I'm not allowed to watch TV at all for the next two weeks, thanks to that note from Mrs. Harding!" Charlie told Emma and Lindsey as they walked through the Eastbridge shopping mall on their way to Miss Claudine's School of Ballet.

"You could come to my house some days and watch it," Lindsey offered sympathetically.

"Mine, too," said Emma.

Charlie threw her arms around both of them. "Oh, thank you, thank you," she sighed.

The girls arrived at Miss Claudine's and made their way into the narrow dressing room. There they began pulling on their baby-blue leotards and pink tights. Other girls from their class were busy tying their pink ballet slippers or pulling their hair back into tight buns or braids.

Primping in the mirror was Danielle Sainte-Marie, a pretty girl with long dark hair coiled neatly into a bun. Danielle wore a black leotard and tights, since she really belonged in intermediate ballet. She came early to help with the beginners' class and to spend more time with her idol, their teacher, Miss Claudine.

"*Honk, honk!*" Danielle jumped. Emma had come up quietly behind her and was honking loudly in her ear.

"Have you lost your mind?" Danielle asked icily.

"I was just practicing to be one of your swan slaves," Emma said, tossing her head. Teasing Danielle was one of Emma's favorite pastimes.

"For your information, swans do not honk," Danielle told her, turning back to the mirror. "Geese honk."

"I heard swans honk once," Lindsey chimed in. "They sound a little different from geese, though. They make a sound more like *ha-onnk, ha-onnnnnk ha-onnnnnk* !"

"No, I think it's faster than that," Charlie said. "It's more like, *honkhonkhonkhonk*!"

The three girls gathered around Danielle and performed their version of swans honking. Danielle covered her ears with her hands. "Stop it!" she yelled. The girls quieted down, biting their lips to keep from exploding with laughter. "These swans do not honk," Danielle told them angrily. "They're magical swans."

"Oh, right. Magical," laughed Emma.

Danielle glared at her. "Everything's a big joke to you, isn't it?" she said, hands on her hips.

"Not everything," replied Emma with a devious grin. "Only the things that are too silly to take seriously." She looked right at Danielle.

Flushed with anger, the older girl whirled around and stomped out of the dressing room.

"I can't stand that girl," muttered Emma as she stood in front of the mirror and applied purple shadow to her lids. Now that she was eleven, her mother let her wear a little mascara and lip gloss. That wasn't enough for Emma, though, who applied even more makeup once she was out of the house— and took it off before returning home.

"No kidding," said Lindsey, standing behind Emma and running her fingers through her medium-length curly blond hair. "I'd never have guessed."

The girls went out into the studio to begin class. Some of the other ballet students were already lined up at the practice barre, warming up for class by bending down and grabbing their ankles. Others sat on the floor, stretching out over their widespread legs. Miss Claudine had taught them these exercises to help them prepare their muscles for the hard work of dancing.

"Bonjour, mesdemoiselles," Miss Claudine greeted them brightly as she strode briskly into the studio, her long ash blond braid bouncing behind her. Charlie, Emma, and Lindsey checked, as always, to see what their teacher was wearing. Miss Claudine seemed to have an almost endless supply of dance wear in different colors and styles. Today she wore a sea green leotard and matching tights, with a short, fringed purple dance skirt around her hips. The colors made her sharp blue eyes appear an even deeper blue than usual.

"We will begin," she said. The class knew the routine. They lined up at the barre and waited for Miss Claudine to place a classical record on her scratchy record player. Then she led them through a series of pliés in the different ballet positions.

Charlie, Emma, and Lindsey had just about mastered the pliés, except for the grand pliés in fifth position, where their feet were one in front of the other. The grand pliés still made them topple off balance.

"Find your center," Miss Claudine coached. Charlie knew she meant their center of balance, but she wasn't exactly sure how to go about finding it. She hoped that on the magical day when she finally found her center, all the other ballet techniques would fall into place. But right now she imagined running an ad in the local paper that read: *Missing, one center. Beginning ballet student will pay any price. If found, please call Charlie Clark.*

Wherever her center was, Charlie knew now that she hadn't found it. She wobbled horribly with almost every move. Arabesques, which required her to lift her back leg off the ground and lean forward, made her shake all over. Even though she was holding onto the barre, it didn't help much. Freestanding moves, done in the middle of the room without the support of the barre, were a total disaster.

Today, while practicing freestanding arabesques, Charlie lost her balance and fell to the side, pushing a girl named Tish over as well. "Miss Claudine," Tish whined, picking herself up off the floor, "do I have to stand next to her? She knocks me over all the time."

Charlie wanted to protest, but what Tish said was

13

true. This wasn't the first time she'd brought Tish down with her. For that matter, on different occasions she'd sent a number of her other classmates sprawling as well.

Miss Claudine smoothed the top of her hair with her long, delicate hand, a sure sign that she was thinking. Ignoring Tish, she walked over to Charlie. "Let's work on finding your center a moment, shall we, Mademoiselle Charlotte?"

Charlie was so mortified that she didn't even bother to correct Miss Claudine, who insisted on calling her by her real name, Charlotte. Charlie hated it, but Miss Claudine said it was a wonderful French name.

Miss Claudine guided Charlie's back leg up while she steadied her hips with her free hand. "Steady, steady," she said calmly. "Breathe slowly. Use your tummy muscles."

Charlie tried to concentrate. She sucked her stomach in tightly and held her breath. "You're forgetting to breathe," Miss Claudine instructed as Charlie's supporting leg wobbled violently.

Charlie heard the sound of girls giggling and caught the words, "She can't even breathe right," whispered amid the tittering laughter. Embarrassed, her concentration broke and Charlie teetered out of Miss Claudine's hands.

"You are too tense," Miss Claudine said. "Relax."

"I'll try," said Charlie, rolling her eyes. It was easy for Miss Claudine to say. She didn't have a whole class full of girls giggling and staring at her.

"All right, mesdemoiselles," said Miss Claudine, turning to the rest of the class. "You *all* need to work

on this." Together, the class ran through arabesques and other steps which Miss Claudine said they'd need when they performed the scene from *Swan Lake*. Charlie, Lindsey, and Emma knew that Miss Claudine planned a final recital. But that wasn't until June, and it seemed a long way away.

Charlie's legs were beginning to ache when Miss Claudine finally announced it was time for ballet culture. That was the part of ballet class Emma, Charlie, and Lindsey liked best. The students would all sit on the floor around Miss Claudine, and she would tell them the story of a different ballet. Each story came alive with her dramatic style of storytelling.

"Today, rather than tell the story of a ballet, I want to talk about Eastbridge Day," Miss Claudine told the class, taking a seat on a folding chair in the center of the circle. "I just received a flyer saying that in two weeks, on Saturday, the mall will have a very special day where all the different shops will display their goods. Davidson's Jewelry will show how they make their glazed earrings. Miss Lilly's Beauty Salon will do make-overs. All the small stores will give demonstrations."

Emma, Charlie, and Lindsey exchanged worried glances. They didn't like the sound of this. "So does that mean class is canceled?" asked Lindsey, hoping that was what Miss Claudine was getting at.

"*Au contraire, chérie!*" exclaimed Miss Claudine. "This class will be very much a part of the festivities. We have been assigned a place near the reflecting pool in the center of the mall. All my classes will perform

16

scenes from great ballets. You will perform our scene from *Swan Lake*."

Charlie felt as if a dying fish was flapping around inside her stomach. "In front of everybody at the mall?" she asked.

"But of course," said Miss Claudine happily. "I know it's a bit sudden, but we have been practicing the scene. Why not show the world how talented you all are? Performance is the ultimate goal for all these lessons, is it not?"

It certainly wasn't Charlie's ultimate goal, but she nodded her head in agreement. This was terrible. The three girls looked at one another with horror-filled eyes. Perform in public?

"We will have costumes and scenery," Miss Claudine continued enthusiastically. "We'll have to work very hard, but it will be truly wonderful. And you know, Danielle, we will be counting on you in the role of Odette, the Swan Princess."

"I won't let you down, Miss Claudine!" Danielle answered, beaming with pride.

"Are all the classes performing?" Emma asked. "I think the older classes would do a much better job than we would."

"The advanced classes will be performing as well. But the performance of the beginners is, in many ways, most important. I need the audience to be inspired by the beginners' class. That way new students will enroll for next session. Most of the students in the upper classes started here as beginners."

"Nice try," whispered Lindsey to Emma. When Miss Claudine dismissed class, Emma, Lindsey, and

Charlie trudged back toward the dressing room wearing sullen expressions. "I am just simply going to die of total embarrassment," Lindsey wailed. "What if someone from school sees us? How humiliating!"

"You!" cried Emma. "What about me? I'll feel like a twit in a tutu stumbling over my own feet."

"Neither of you is as bad as I am," said Charlie. She looked at her two friends, who nodded sadly back at her.

"You're not supposed to agree with me!" Charlie exploded. "You're supposed to say, 'Oh, no. We're much worse than you are, Charlie.'"

"Do you want us to lie?" asked Lindsey.

"I guess not," Charlie admitted glumly. The girls changed their clothing without much conversation. Each was busy imagining herself making some terrible blunder in front of a crowd of people who would then laugh uproariously. And Charlie couldn't get Lindsey's words out of her mind. What if someone from school *did* see them? What if that someone was named Mark Johnson? Charlie felt that flip-floppy feeling in her stomach once again.

They pulled on their jackets and picked up their dance bags. As they came into the front room they noticed that Miss Claudine had opened the pink curtain that usually covered the plate glass front of the store. They knew she sometimes did this to encourage interest in the school from passersby.

This time she had generated interest, but not the kind that would do the school any good. A group of boys from Eastbridge Elementary stood peering in. Some were simply looking. Others had squashed

18

themselves up against the glass and were making goofy faces at the girls inside.

A group of girls from the beginners' class stood inside by the window, pointing and laughing at the boys. Charlie stopped short. Standing behind one of the boys pressed against the glass was Mark Johnson. She was glad to see him—and she wanted to run away at the same time.

Standing very close to Emma and Lindsey, Charlie walked out the front door with her friends. Half of her wanted Mark to say something to her. The other half wanted to slip by unnoticed.

"Hey, Munson," yelled a boy named Timmy Traub, "you going to play volleyball with us next week? Mr. Hyers says he'll leave the net up and he'll hang around if we want to play."

"Maybe," Lindsey answered, stopping. She was confident that although she was small, she was the best volleyball player in the fifth grade. "Probably."

"You're on my team, then. Okay?" said Timmy.

"Okay," Lindsey agreed. "And you know who else you should try to get . . ." While Lindsey and Timmy planned their future super team, Emma and Charlie stood off to the side and waited uncomfortably.

As they waited, Danielle came out the front door, wearing a long gray cardigan sweater over her black leotard. She always went and got a snack for herself and Miss Claudine in between classes. She seemed totally unembarrassed about being seen in her leotard. Even Emma had to admit she looked pretty good in it with her trim, graceful figure.

Charlie was distracted from watching Danielle

wiggle across the mall by an approaching figure. It was Mark Johnson! He was coming over to talk to her!

"Hi," he said to both Charlie and Emma. "Listen, I wanted to say I'm sorry we acted so dumb about your report the other day."

Charlie felt her hands shake nervously. She hoped her anxiety didn't show. "It's okay. I knew you guys were kidding around."

"It was a pretty funny report, in a way," he continued. "Better than some of the other boring ones."

"Thanks," Charlie said, gazing up at him dreamily. She was mesmerized by the blueness of his eyes and the dimple in his chin.

Mark moved closer to Charlie and lowered his voice. "Can I ask you something?"

"Go ahead, ask," she replied nervously.

"Who was that cute girl who just left? The one in the leotard. I've seen her around school."

"You mean Danielle?" Charlie had to stop her voice from rising shrilly. Emma made a face in disbelief.

"I guess so. That's a pretty name—Danielle." Mark's eyes got a faraway look as he repeated Danielle's name.

Charlie thought she was going to throw up. Mark liked Danielle!

Chapter Three

"What if everyone at school finds out about this performance?" asked Charlie as she, Emma, and Lindsey headed through the front door of Eastbridge Elementary.

"No one is going to find out," Lindsey said.

"Well, some kids might see us on Eastbridge Day, but not the whole school," added Emma.

Charlie stopped and picked up a piece of white paper from a stack on a small table in the front hallway of the school. The table was where all flyers and announcements were usually available. As Charlie read the paper, her rosy complexion went pale. "Nobody's going to find out, huh!" she said.

Lindsey and Emma read over her shoulder. The paper featured a cutout Xeroxed photo of Danielle dressed in a tutu and *en pointe*. Above the photo were the words: Don't Miss *Swan Lake*! Starring Danielle Sainte-Marie and others from Eastbridge Elementary

School. February 10 at Twelve O'Clock by the Reflecting Pool in the Eastbridge Mall.

"I don't believe this," muttered Charlie.

Emma grabbed the stack of papers and stuffed them into her oversized tapestry pocketbook.

"You can't do that," whispered Lindsey, looking around to make sure no one was watching.

"Well, I'm doing it," said Emma defiantly.

"Oh, no, look!" cried Charlie. She pointed down the hall. There was a small pile of the white flyers stacked at the doorway of every classroom.

"The bell's going to ring in three minutes," said Emma, checking her purple plastic watch. "We'd better hurry." Without another word, the girls began gathering up the papers.

The halls were becoming busy as students and teachers headed into their classrooms. Mrs. Kneff, their history teacher, looked at them suspiciously. "Mr. O'Neill asked us to pick these up," Charlie told her, referring to the principal. "He said they were a fire hazard."

Mrs. Kneff raised an eyebrow doubtfully. "Put them back on the front hall table, and don't be late for your first class," she warned sternly.

"Yes, Mrs. Kneff," Charlie agreed in a respectful voice.

Just then, the bell rang. The three girls met in the middle of the hallway, clutching the papers to their chests. "I looked, and the entire hall around the corner is filled with these things," Lindsey whispered urgently.

"Well, at least we can get rid of these," said Charlie, stuffing her flyers into a hallway trash basket.

"Quick! I hear someone coming," Emma said. "Run into the girls' room and we'll get the rest of them after homeroom starts." She headed for the girls' bathroom, and Charlie and Lindsey followed. There, they each went into a separate booth and sat cross-legged on the toilet seats so that if a hall monitor or teacher checked, there would be no telltale feet to give them away.

Charlie sat there and looked down at the fliers. This was really terrible. Now the whole school would be there to see her trip over her own two feet!

There was a quick rap on her stall door. "Let's go," Emma whispered. "But leave your jackets in here, so no one will know we haven't been to homeroom yet." They piled their jackets on the windowsill and stuffed the flyers they'd collected so far into the trash can. Then they opened the bathroom door carefully.

"Okay, come on," said Emma, and the three of them scurried down the hall, half sliding around the corner of the smooth, waxed marble floor. They stopped short in the hallway, their mouths hanging open in dismay. All the flyers were gone.

Emma slapped her own forehead lightly with the palm of her hand. "We weren't thinking," she said. "Of course. All the teachers picked up the flyers on the way into class."

"And they're probably giving them out right now," added Lindsey mournfully. "We'll just have to wear bags over our heads for the rest of the year."

"Quiet, quiet," Emma shushed her. "I'm thinking." She screwed up her features into an expression of deep concentration and sighed deeply. She closed her eyes and sighed again. "Okay, I've got it," she said at last. "We'll go in, two at a time, and say Mr. O'Neill sent us to get the flyers."

"But why?" asked Lindsey.

"Because there's an error!" offered Charlie.

"Good!" Emma agreed. "We'll say the flyers have the wrong day printed on them." The three girls stood in front of the first door. Emma knocked. "Charlie and I will go in first, but after this we're taking turns."

Lindsey ducked back quickly as Miss Miles came to the door. Emma explained about the misprinted flyers. "Very well," Miss Miles agreed. "Class, please pass back those papers I just gave you," she instructed the class.

Charlie's hands trembled as she took the papers from Miss Miles. She felt as if she had the word *liar* written all over her face. But if she did, Miss Miles didn't seem to notice.

At the next classroom, neither Lindsey nor Charlie could get up the nerve to make the speech about the misprints, so Emma finally agreed to do all the talking, with Lindsey and Charlie taking turns standing beside her.

Within fifteen minutes they'd collected all the flyers. "That was a brilliant plan," Lindsey congratulated Emma as they walked back down the hall and turned the corner, heading toward the girls' room. Their arms were overflowing with slightly mashed flyers.

"I hope you have another plan," whispered Charlie. "Look who's coming."

Coming down the hall was Mr. O'Neill himself. He put his hand to his brown-rimmed glasses and focused on the girls. Then he pushed back his brown tweed jacket and put his hands on his hips. "Ladies, may I ask what you are doing in the hallway?" he asked.

"We're . . . ummm . . . collecting these flyers," Emma answered, a slight quiver in her voice.

Mr. O'Neill reached out and Emma handed him a flyer. "May I ask why?" he said, inspecting the paper. All three girls began to explain about the supposed misprint.

He ran his hand through his blond hair. "Okay, okay. Who sent you for these?"

Charlie, Emma, and Lindsey looked at one another anxiously. "Nobody, really," Emma spoke up. "We just saw the mistake and we didn't want everyone going to the mall on the wrong day."

"So you don't have hall passes," said the principal. The girls shook their heads. Mr. O'Neill took a small pink pad from the inside pocket of his jacket. Detention slips. He handed each of them one. "Give me those flyers, and I'll walk you to homeroom."

With slumped shoulders, they followed him back to their homeroom. Mr. Ramos, their teacher, looked at them sternly as they entered the classroom and took their seats. "Maryellen found your coats in the ladies' room. They're now on your seats," was all he said.

They didn't have a chance to talk to one another

until the lunch bell rang later in the day. Then they walked together toward the cafeteria. "I can't believe we got detention," grumbled Lindsey. "And all because of that stupid Danielle."

As the girls neared the cafeteria, Emma let out a small gasp. "I don't believe this!" she cried. There, at the front entrance of the cafeteria, was Danielle. And she was greeting each student with a smile and a flyer.

Not knowing what to say, the girls glared at Danielle as they passed her on their way into the cafeteria. Charlie looked across the large, bustling room and saw that a group of boys from her class had folded the flyers into paper airplanes and were sailing them across the tables at one another. Some of the other boys had ripped up the paper and rolled it into wet spitballs. They were using their straws to shoot the small soggy balls of paper at some girls next to them.

At the table beside her, a group of girls had torn the paper into thin strips and were using them to make braided paper bracelets. Beside them, some of their classmates were making use of the back of the paper to play tic-tac-toe.

Charlie decided this was all very encouraging. "No one is even reading the flyers!" she told Emma and Lindsey.

Then she caught sight of Mark Johnson sitting at the end of the table with the tic-tac-toe group. He was staring wide-eyed at the flyer, studying it as if it were the most fascinating thing he'd ever read.

She watched as he got up and went over to Danielle at the doorway. He appeared to be asking her a question, his head bowed shyly as he spoke. From the enthusiastic look on Danielle's face, Charlie could tell she was telling him all about the performance. She saw Mark nod his head yes.

Yes, he would be there. What else could he possibly be saying? The thought made Charlie put down her tuna sandwich. Somehow she wasn't hungry anymore. Mark Johnson was going to be there to see every humiliating moment of her performance.

She mashed her lunch down into her brown bag. "Let's go out into the schoolyard," she suggested.

"Too cold," grumbled Emma.

"Hey, Charlie," someone shouted. She turned. It was Mark Johnson.

"I'm going to come see your show," he called happily.

Charlie looked around quickly, hoping no one had heard him. "Great," she muttered nervously. "Just great."

Chapter Four

"Now try it one more time," said Miss Claudine. Charlie pressed her lips into a long, straight grimace and heaved a sigh. The class was practicing the third arabesque position, which they would need for their performance of *Swan Lake*. Charlie always had trouble with arabesques, and this one, with one leg off the ground and both arms held out in front, invariably sent her pitching forward, flailing her arms wildly to keep from falling face first onto the floor.

Miss Claudine had stopped the whole class to go over the move with her—and over, and over, and over it. At least that's how it felt to Charlie. Though she was looking at Miss Claudine, Charlie sensed the class was growing impatient. She imagined them all standing around, their arms folded, staring at her with annoyed expressions and tapping their feet irritably.

A quick look told her that a few girls were standing in exactly that position, but most were whispering together or fixing their hair in the mirror. Emma and Lindsey were busy playing thumbsies, each one trying to press the other's thumb down first. Still, Charlie felt pressured to get the step right this time.

She attempted the arabesque and went skittering forward. Trying desperately to balance herself, she put her extended leg down—and her ankle turned painfully beneath her. In a second she was on the ground. "Oooohhhhh," she groaned, grabbing her ankle.

Miss Claudine knelt down quickly beside her. "Sit back, *chérie,* and let me have a look." Gently she rotated the sore ankle. "Try to move it yourself," she instructed.

Wincing with pain, Charlie turned her ankle in a small circle. "It hurts a lot," she told her teacher truthfully.

"Yes, but you can move it, so I doubt it's broken." Miss Claudine lifted Charlie to her feet and supported her as she hopped over to a chair in the corner. "Wait one moment and I will get you an Ace bandage," she said, running out to the front room.

"Are you okay?" asked Lindsey, who had come over with Emma.

"It really hurts."

Emma leaned in close. "Does it really? Or did you just get sick of doing arabesques?" she whispered.

"No, it really, really hurts," Charlie answered.

Miss Claudine returned with the Ace bandage. "Come with me to the dressing room and we'll get those tights off and wrap the ankle," she said, helping Charlie up from the chair.

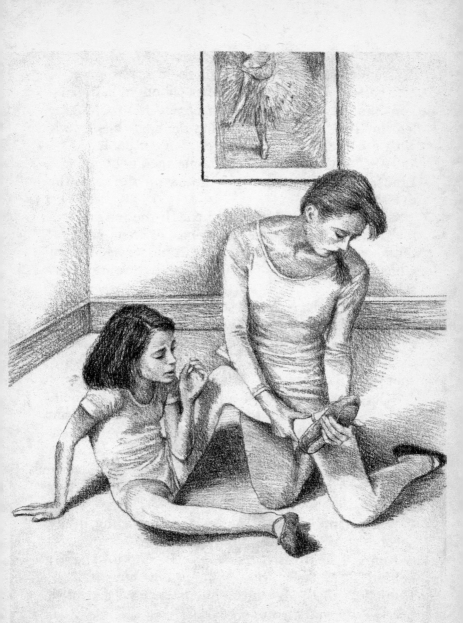

After class, Emma and Lindsey found Charlie dressed and sitting in the front room reading a copy of a ballet magazine which Miss Claudine had given her. She got up, leaning on a cane. "Miss Claudine lent me this," she said, showing them the black cane with a carved wooden handle. "Isn't it cool?"

"We'll get dressed fast and come back to help you," Lindsey offered as she and Emma hurried into the dressing room.

Charlie sat and thumbed through the magazine a few minutes more. The ballerinas in their graceful outfits were very beautiful. Miss Claudine had taught Charlie to like ballet—she just didn't like doing it herself.

Danielle walked by and stopped in front of Charlie, shaking her head. Charlie tried to appear engrossed in the magazine, but she could feel Danielle staring down at her. "What do you want?" she finally snapped.

"I'm looking to see if your nose grew," Danielle said in a very superior tone of voice. "You know what I mean. Remember how Pinocchio's nose grew whenever he lied?"

"For your information, I am *not* lying," Charlie said in her snottiest voice. "Ask Miss Claudine. My ankle is all swollen."

"Sure, sure," said Danielle, her lip curling into a sneer.

Emma had dressed quickly and came up silently behind Danielle. "You should know how it feels, Danielle," she said, "since you *always* have a swollen head. Why don't you go soak it?"

"Ha, ha, ha," Danielle said sourly, and then, lifting her nose in the air, she stomped off into the dressing room.

Lindsey joined them, and the three girls made their way out of Miss Claudine's and up to the mall parking lot, where Lindsey's father was waiting to drive them home. "That Danielle is such a twit," complained Lindsey as she helped Charlie into the car.

"She said I was faking, but I'm not, you know," said Charlie.

"We know," Lindsey assured her.

Charlie's mother was on the kitchen phone when she walked in the back door. "I'll call you back later, Sue," Mrs. Clark said hurriedly when she saw Charlie limp toward her. "What happened?" she asked, pulling a kitchen chair out for her daughter.

"I told you that you shouldn't have forced me to take ballet," Charlie said pitifully. She explained all about her inability to master the third arabesque position and the resulting injury.

"Miss Claudine says it isn't broken, but it hurts an awful lot." Suddenly tears welled up in Charlie's eyes, and she let them run down her cheeks. She wasn't sure if she was crying because her ankle *did* hurt her, or because she was frustrated at always being the worst in the class. Or maybe because she would have to perform in front of Mark Johnson—whom she was trying not to think about. It was all so hopeless! Charlie buried her face in her hands and wept loudly.

Her mother pulled a kitchen chair up and put her arms around Charlie. "It was a bad morning, huh," she said sympathetically.

33

Charlie nodded through her tears and then turned and continued to sob into her mother's shoulder. She wasn't ready to tell her about all the things that were bothering her, but it felt good to be held.

When her crying died down, her mother handed her a napkin from the holder on the kitchen table. She wiped her eyes and then blew her nose. Just then, Frank, the oldest of her three brothers, came in. "Hey, what's the matter, squirt?" he asked.

"I hurt my ankle, and don't call me squirt." Charlie sniffled, wiping her eyes one last time with the back of her hands.

"Let's have a look," he said, his blue eyes twinkling enthusiastically. He squatted and gingerly lifted her leg onto his knees. Frank was captain of the Eastbridge High varsity football team, and injuries fascinated him. He wanted to study to become a chiropractor specializing in sports medicine after he graduated from high school in June. "Whoever wrapped this bandage did a great job," he said, taking off the sock Miss Claudine had put over the bandage.

"Watch it, that hurts," Charlie snapped.

"I'll bet it does," Frank said, unwrapping the bandage. "It's super-swollen." He turned to his mother. "I think you'd better take her to the doctor."

"Miss Claudine says it's not broken," Charlie said quickly.

"Probably not, but you know there are lots of small bones in your feet. And you might have torn a muscle. You can't be too careful with feet," Frank replied. Charlie knew that Frank held feet in high regard. He was always discussing how different sneakers supported the arch or the ankle and pondering which brand of sneaker was best for which sport. Every time he got some money he ran out and bought another pair. Charlie figured he had almost ten pairs of sneakers.

"I'll see if Dr. Janklow can take us today," said her mother, flipping through the pages of her phone directory. "I'm not sure what kind of hours she has on Saturday."

"I'm proud of you, squirt," said Frank. "You have your very first sports injury."

"Thanks, Frank," Charlie muttered. "Thanks loads."

Two hours later, Charlie found herself in the crowded waiting room of her family doctor's office. "All right, Charlie, Mrs. Clark, you're next," said the nurse. She rose and opened the door to the doctor's inner office.

Dr. Janklow was a short, white-haired woman with a jolly manner. She had Charlie hop onto the examining table, then she unwrapped her Ace bandage. She felt Charlie's bare foot with her strong hands. "Yes, all right. Good. Uh-huh," she muttered as she pressed and flexed different parts of Charlie's foot. "Good news," she announced at last. "You have a slight sprain, but nothing is torn or broken. Keep it up for a day or two. Soak it in warm water or use a heating pad to relieve the pain. In a day or two, three at the most, you should be fine."

"Do I need the bandage?" Charlie asked.

"If you want some support when you have to move, it's fine."

"Could I have crutches?" Charlie had always wanted crutches, ever since Reva Harris had them for three episodes of *Search for Love*.

Dr. Janklow laughed. "I think that handsome cane you have there should be sufficient." Mrs. Clark got up and thanked the doctor. "Are you too old for a lollipop, Charlie?" Dr. Janklow asked.

Charlie hesitated. "I think so," she finally answered, straightening her shoulders.

"Well, take one anyway," Dr. Janklow said with a wink, pressing a red pop into her hand.

Charlie smiled. "Thanks." Dr. Janklow had even remembered she liked the red ones best.

Mrs. Clark insisted that Charlie sit in the backseat of their blue hatchback so that she could keep her foot up. When they got home, her mother propped her up with pillows on the living room couch and handed her the remote control to the TV. Charlie smiled at her mother, knowing that she was going out of her way to make her feel better. She flipped around the dial and clicked past the sports shows until she found an old horror movie in black and white.

A good smell wafted in from the kitchen. Charlie sniffed and realized her mother was making a roast chicken, one of her favorite meals. She snuggled down into her pillows. Saturday-evening TV and roast chicken cooking in the kitchen—life had its terrible moments, but this was one of the better times. She flexed her ankle and realized that it didn't hurt half as much as it had that afternoon. There was a dull ache, but not the throbbing pain she'd had before.

Her brother Harry came in, followed a half hour later by her brother John. Each took a turn examining her ankle. And each time she told them the story of her injury, Charlie remembered it as being worse and worse. By the time she told the story to her father, she imagined that her poor ankle had been blown up to the size of a melon, and Dr. Janklow had looked faint at the sight of it. "But it's not as swollen now," she told her father with a pained smile. "Even though it still hurts."

Mr. Clark ruffled his daughter's hair affectionately. "That's my brave girl," he said. "I sprained my ankle once and I know how much it hurts. Just take it easy and watch some television."

Her father was telling her to watch TV! And he thought she was brave! Charlie sighed happily.

At dinnertime her mother set up a tray next to the couch and let her continue to watch as she ate her chicken, mashed potatoes, string beans, and cranberry sauce. After supper, Charlie got to pick the programs they'd all watch while her father sat at the other end of the couch and held a heating pad on her ankle.

As Charlie was getting ready for bed that night, she realized happily that her ankle felt much better. She had just crawled under the covers when her mother knocked on her bedroom door and stuck her head in. "How does the ankle feel?" she asked, a concerned look in her eyes.

Charlie was about to say it hardly hurt at all—but something stopped her. "Pretty bad," she lied. "I think it's getting worse."

Her mother looked worried. "Well, maybe after a good night's sleep you'll feel better," she said. She sat on the bed next to Charlie and gently pulled back the covers to look at her ankle. "The swelling's gone down."

"Maybe, but the pain is worse," Charlie insisted.

Her mother pulled the covers back up and kissed Charlie on the forehead. "Try to get some sleep," she said.

Charlie said good night as her mother flipped off the lamp by her bed. She rolled onto her side and stared at the patch of moonlight that shone into the room from under her half-closed shade. She felt terrible about lying, but after *so* many bad days in a row, she didn't want to let go of these good feelings. Not yet, anyway.

That's when it occurred to her. As long as her ankle was injured, she wouldn't have to go to ballet class. And she wouldn't have to be in *Swan Lake.*

Chapter Five

"Now, mesdemoiselles, look at Danielle with love and concern on your faces," instructed Miss Claudine. "She is your princess and she is dying. A ballerina is not only a dancer, she is an actress, as well."

Emma and Lindsey exchanged glances. "All I want to do is throw up when I look at her," whispered Emma. She and Lindsey were rehearsing the *Swan Lake* scene along with the rest of the class. As the Swan Princess, Danielle was fluttering around the room, pretending she'd just been shot with an arrow. The other girls, playing her swan attendants, were standing in a semicircle behind Danielle, trying to look upset.

"You are as stiff as statues," Miss Claudine scolded. "Let me see graceful swans, not stuffed pigeons."

"Boy, she's in a bad mood today," whispered Lindsey. "I've never seen her act this crabby."

"Charlie's lucky," Emma whispered back, starting

to wobble as she stood in position, her hands crossed in front and one leg behind the other. "It's been a whole week and her ankle still isn't better. If she misses one more class, she won't even have to be in this dumb show."

"I know, but it doesn't seem the same without—"

"Mesdemoiselles Emma and Lindsey," Miss Claudine cut Lindsey off crossly. "There will be no whispering in the corps de ballet. Magical swans do not whisper."

"Sorry, Miss Claudine," the girls answered together. They knew they shouldn't have been whispering, but still, Miss Claudine did seem extremely tense today.

Usually it was almost impossible to upset her. It was as if Miss Claudine wrapped herself in the beauty and enchantment of the ballet. It normally took a lot to get her angry.

Today there were circles under her alert blue eyes, and everything seemed to irritate her. She'd even snapped at Danielle.

Miss Claudine looked at her thin gold watch. "We will not have ballet culture this week," she told the class. "We need to continue our practice. Eastbridge Day is next Saturday."

She ran them through another half hour of practice, sighing when she adjusted the position of their feet and hands. Even Danielle seemed to lose some of her zeal as she fluttered to the floor for what seemed like the hundredth time that day.

"All right," Miss Claudine said at last in a weary

voice. "I will see you on Wednesday. *Au revoir, chéries.*"

Emma and Lindsey headed for the door of the studio, but Miss Claudine stopped them. "How is Mademoiselle Charlotte?" she asked.

"Not so good," Lindsey told her. "The doctor said her ankle was just sprained, but it doesn't seem to be getting any better. Her mother is going to take her for X rays if it doesn't stop hurting in the next few days."

Miss Claudine pursed her lips thoughtfully. "I'd hate for her to miss out on the fun of the show, but she's missed two rehearsals now. I don't know what to do."

"She'd understand if you said she couldn't be in the show," said Emma. "I'm almost positive she wouldn't mind."

The teacher smoothed back her hair with both hands, a sure sign that she was trying to figure something out. "No," she said, "she would mind. She might not realize that she minded, but later on it would be a missed experience—one that she would regret."

Miss Claudine cocked her head to one side, still thinking. "Tell Mademoiselle Charlotte that if her foot feels better by Wednesday, she should come to class for rehearsal. I'll put her in the back line of the chorus. The most important thing is that she have the experience. That is even more important than the performance itself." She walked away from them looking preoccupied, as though she were very deep in thought.

"She's acting strange today," Emma remarked.

"It was nice of her to let Charlie stay in the show, though."

"I don't think Charlie will be too happy about it," said Emma as they headed toward the dressing room.

"I know what you mean," Lindsey said. "I don't want to make a jerk of myself in this show, either, but Charlie seems to turn green at the mention of it. It's like it really makes her sick. It must be because she's so bad. I'm not trying to be mean. I'm just saying the truth, between us."

Emma headed into the dressing room first and squirmed out of her leotard. "It could be that," she said, "but I think there's more. I think she has a crush on Mark Johnson and she's worried that he'll be there on Eastbridge Day to see her goof up."

"She likes Mark Johnson!" Lindsey gasped, stunned. Lindsey liked boys for playing sports and hanging around with, but she had never considered *liking* a boy. And if any one of them was going to start liking boys she'd have assumed it would be Emma, with her generally more grown-up ways—not Charlie.

"You don't have to look so shocked," said Emma.

Lindsey took off her leotard and ran her fingers through her curly hair. "Is there anyone you like?"

"Not since I moved here," Emma said, wiggling into her black stretch pants. "But I had a boyfriend when I lived in the city."

"You did?" Lindsey said in disbelief.

"Sure. Kip Livingston. He was real cute." Emma

pulled on her oversized T-shirt. "It's no big deal to have a boyfriend."

"Does Mark Johnson like Charlie, do you think?" asked Lindsey, sitting on the bench and tying her sneakers.

Emma shook her head as she rubbed off her eye makeup with a wet tissue. "You won't believe this, but he likes Danielle. Tish told me. Mark is friends with her brother."

"This is all too strange for me," said Lindsey, getting to her feet and stuffing her ballet things into her bag. She looked around the dressing room. Everyone else had changed and gone. "Come on. Your mother's probably already in the parking lot waiting," she urged Emma.

The girls headed to the front area of the dressing room, but Emma stopped short in the doorway. She pulled on Lindsey's jacket to stop her, as well. "Adrian's out there with Miss Claudine," she whispered.

"So what?" Lindsey whispered back, peeking out at Miss Claudine's handsome blond boyfriend who stood beside their teacher at the front desk. "What's so strange about that?"

"Look at him. He's got his arms around her, and I think she's crying," Emma said, taking another step back from the doorway.

Alarmed, Lindsey stepped back beside her. The girls stood silently and listened. At first it was hard to hear Miss Claudine, who murmured something in a tearful voice, but Adrian's deep voice was easy to make out. "It's probably not as bad as you think,

44

Claudine," he said soothingly. "And even if the performance is awful, so what? They're just kids."

"You haven't been listening to me," Miss Claudine said, her voice rising with exasperation. "It does matter. The new session starts in two weeks and I have only one new student signed up. Five of my advanced students are graduating, two intermediates are dropping out, and four of my beginners have told me they won't be back for different reasons. I can't afford to keep the doors open with so few students. I'm barely paying the bills now."

"You could raise tuition," Adrian suggested.

"Oh, I hate to do that," she said, wiping her eyes with the back of her delicate hand.

"Maybe you need to advertise."

"Advertising costs money," she said, looking up at him. "This performance is a perfect form of advertisement. But I'm afraid it will backfire. Danielle needs much more work, and the corps is a shambles. None of the girls seem to take it seriously. It's my fault, really. I suppose I've rushed them."

"It'll be all right," Adrian told her, rubbing Miss Claudine's shoulders.

"It won't be all right if I have to close the school," she replied, her voice growing quivery. "Teaching is everything to me. What will I do? Get a job as a saleswoman in a store?"

Emma and Lindsey looked at one another. Miss Claudine a saleswoman? Not able to teach! It was a horrible thought.

"You could teach in another school," Adrian told her.

Miss Claudine rose angrily. "I've put my whole life into *this* school," she snapped. "In another school they wouldn't let me do things my way. They might not let me bring each student along at his or her own speed."

It grew quiet and Lindsey peeked around the doorway. She saw that Miss Claudine had covered her face with her hands. When she took them away, her eyes and nose were red from crying. "I'm sorry for being angry, *mon cheri,*" she said to Adrian. "But this school is everything to me. Everything."

The sound of a sniff made Lindsey look back over her shoulder. Emma's eyes were red and filled with tears. "Poor Miss Claudine," she murmured, looking at the ceiling to keep her tears from spilling over.

"Yeah," Lindsey agreed sadly.

"Let me go into the office and freshen up," they heard Miss Claudine say. "Danielle will be back from getting our snack momentarily, and my intermediate students will be arriving soon."

Adrian told her he'd be back to pick her up after class. The squeaking of Miss Claudine's office door told Emma and Lindsey that she'd gone inside.

The girls quickly ran through the front office and walked silently up the stairs to the top level of the mall. "Now I feel really bad for whispering during rehearsal," said Emma as they neared the back door, where Emma's mother would be waiting.

"I feel terrible for calling her a crab," Lindsey agreed.

Outside the mall, the winter sky was overcast. Flat gray-black clouds streaked the sky, and a damp chill sent a shiver through them. They spotted Mrs. Guthrie's sporty green Jaguar parked several spots away from them and headed toward it.

"I know I always complain about ballet class and all," said Emma. "But I'd really hate it if Miss Claudine had to close down. I guess I'd kind of . . . miss her."

Lindsey folded her arms against the chill and looked at Emma seriously. "Me, too," she said.

Chapter Six

"Don't tell Charlie about Miss Claudine," Emma said that afternoon as she and Lindsey stood on Charlie's front steps. "It will just make her feel bad, and there's nothing she can do about it with her foot all messed up."

Just then Charlie appeared in the doorway, leaning heavily on her cane. "Come on in," she said, pushing open the storm door.

Lindsey and Emma followed her into the living room. "Don't you ever get sick of that thing?" asked Lindsey, pointing to the TV set where a car commercial was blaring on the screen.

"Nope," Charlie answered, settling back onto the couch.

"Could you at least turn it off while we're here?" Lindsey requested.

"I'll turn the sound off, okay?" Charlie aimed the remote at the set and clicked off the volume. "You don't understand. Since I've hurt my ankle, I'm allowed to watch all the TV I want. It won't last for-ever, so I have to take advantage of it while I can."

"How's your foot?" asked Emma.

Charlie's face took on a grim expression. "It hurts a lot. The swelling is all gone, but the pain is unbear-able."

In her heart, Charlie was dying to confide in her friends. She wanted to tell them that her foot was just fine—she just didn't want to admit it yet. All she had to do was hang on until next Wednesday. Then she would have missed all the rehearsals for the *Swan Lake* performance and she couldn't be in the show. Besides, she was enjoying being pampered at home and at school. Everyone made such a fuss, helping her up and down the stairs, excusing her from gym class. And then, of course, there was the unlimited TV. Her parents had lifted all their television restric-tions, saying this was a special situation.

But she couldn't let Emma and Lindsey in on her secret, because then it would seem like a real lie. As it was, she could convince herself that her foot really *did* hurt. If even one other person knew the truth, then her lies would seem more real than they did now with no one knowing the truth. She knew she couldn't stand that feeling.

" . . . and Danielle really thinks she is a princess," Emma was telling her. "The whole thing is just hor-rendously bad."

Emma and Lindsey gave Charlie Miss Claudine's message. "If your foot is better by Wednesday, you can still be in the show," Lindsey told her.

50

"Oh, I doubt it will be better by then," Charlie insisted.

"How can you tell?" Lindsey pressed.

"I just don't think it will be." To change the subject, Charlie picked up the remote and began flipping around the dial. "Hey! Wow! It's Reva Harris!" she cried. The actress who played Reva was on a panel of soap stars who were being interviewed by a blond talk-show host. The only problem was that all their faces were green.

"Darn this stupid TV!" Charlie grumbled as she got up and crossed the room to adjust the color.

Lindsey and Emma looked at one another in surprise. "Doesn't your foot hurt when you do that?" Lindsey asked her.

Charlie was speechless. In her frustration she hadn't even limped. "Umm . . . the pain comes and goes," she stammered.

"Don't lie to us, Charlie Clark," said Emma indignantly. "You're faking!"

"*Shhh!*" Charlie hissed, looking around to make sure none of her family was nearby. "Okay, so what?" she whispered. "It's just until after the show is over."

"You can't do that. It's not fair," said Lindsey. "We have to be in it, so you do, too."

"I do not," Charlie argued. "You're just jealous because I found a way out of it and you haven't." Charlie sat back down on the couch and snapped the TV off.

"Look, Charlie," Emma said calmly, "we understand how you feel, but there's something we have to tell you." She told Charlie what they had over-

heard Miss Claudine saying to Adrian about possibly having to close the school. "And she's counting on us to do a good job on Eastbridge Day, so that other kids will sign up and she won't lose her school. We can't let her down."

"I'd be doing her a favor if I wasn't in the show," said Charlie in a surly tone.

"No, you wouldn't," Lindsey said. "She needs all of us there."

"Miss Claudine says you'd regret missing this experience," added Emma.

Charlie didn't answer them. She sat on the couch with her arms folded tightly across her chest.

"Where's your team spirit?" Lindsey challenged.

Charlie felt trapped. She did want to help Miss Claudine. But she did *not* want to be in the show.

"You're making a big deal out of nothing," Charlie told Emma and Lindsey. "It won't make one bit of difference to Miss Claudine if I'm there."

"But doesn't this make you *want* to be there?" Lindsey insisted. "Miss Claudine has been really nice to us. She's been real patient with—"

"Say it, she's patient with *me,*" Charlie interrupted. "That's because I'm the worst one in the class!"

"The *three* of us are terrible," Emma argued. "You just don't want Mark Johnson to see you."

Charlie's eyes went wide with surprise. "What do you mean?"

"Get off it. I can see how you're always looking at him," Emma told her. "You have a crush on him."

Charlie blushed. "I do not."

"I thought we were your friends," said Lindsey. "How come you're keeping secrets from us all of a sudden?"

"A person is allowed to keep some things to herself once in a while," Charlie answered sulkily.

"Oh, just sit there and watch your stupid old TV until your eyes fall out," said Lindsey angrily as she rose to her feet. "I'm going home."

"Me, too," said Emma, getting out of her chair.

"What are you guys so mad about?" Charlie asked.

"Oh, I'm not really mad," said Lindsey, still scowling. "I just thought you'd care more about Miss Claudine, that's all."

"Don't bother to walk us to the door," said Emma sarcastically. "We know how much your foot hurts."

"Don't worry," said Charlie. "I won't." She pulled a blue couch pillow onto her lap and hit it fiercely with one fist. What right did they have to be so high and mighty with her?

She rolled onto her side and put the pillow under her head. Her mind began to wander, and she pictured Mark Johnson's adorable face. She imagined that he was looking up at her on the stage as she danced her part in *Swan Lake*. Suddenly she stumbled and slid across the stage. There was laughter, and she realized it was Mark's. He was laughing so hard that tears were streaming down his face. Soon the whole audience was laughing hysterically, falling off their chairs and gasping for breath.

Charlie rolled over on the couch and covered her face with a pillow. She wished she could disappear.

"I thought I heard Emma and Lindsey in here," said her mother, walking in from the kitchen.

"They left."

"How's the foot?"

Charlie hesitated. She was tired of lying. But then the image of everyone laughing at her on Eastbridge Day filled her head. She just couldn't do it. "It still hurts," she said.

Her mother looked worried. "It must be very painful," she said seriously. "You've actually turned the TV off."

Chapter Seven

"I can't believe you guys," said Charlie to Emma and Lindsey as they walked out of their last class before lunch.

"Whether you believe it or not, we're going to practice during lunch," Emma told her. "Mrs. Gerald said she'd sit and grade papers while we used her classroom to practice our ballet steps for Saturday. I asked her myself this morning."

"Do you want to come watch?" Lindsey asked.

"What for?" replied Charlie. "Besides, I'm starving."

Leaning heavily on her cane, Charlie made her way down the hall in the opposite direction from Emma and Lindsey. "We'd offer to help you down the stairs, but we're sure you'll be all right without us," Emma said.

Charlie narrowed her eyes and stuck her tongue out at Emma before continuing down the hall. When she reached the top of the stairs, she stood and looked to the bottom. She wanted to walk right down, but she couldn't risk being seen. The teachers would be on the phone to her mother in a second. She knew adults stuck together like that.

"Need some help?" asked a voice right behind her. Charlie turned. It was Mark Johnson!

"Sure, thanks." She smiled at him. Charlie could hardly believe it. It was too good to be true, but it was happening.

He held her elbow with his hand and gently guided her down the steps toward the cafeteria. "I'm not handicapped enough to use the handicapped elevator, and I'm not well enough to get down these stairs," she said, trying to make conversation.

"How long are you going to need that cane?" he asked.

"No one's sure. Probably not much longer."

"That's good," he said. Charlie liked the way the dimple on his chin moved when he spoke.

She let her weight fall against his arm. A lot of boys would have been too embarrassed to help her, but not Mark. Not only was he cute, but he seemed more grown up than most of the boys in the fifth grade.

As they neared the cafeteria, Charlie's delight at walking arm in arm with Mark was ruined by the sight of Danielle standing in front of the doorway with a group of other sixth-grade girls.

She could feel Mark tense up at the sight of Danielle. Charlie hated to think that when he saw Danielle, Mark got the same quivery feeling inside that Charlie felt when she was near him. But it seemed to be true.

"Do you think you can make it the rest of the way on your own?" he asked at the bottom of the stairs.

"Yeah, sure," she answered. Mark didn't seem to notice her glum tone. He smiled at Charlie and then headed toward Danielle.

Charlie hobbled into the cafeteria and took a seat by herself at a table near the door. It was odd not having Emma and Lindsey to sit with. She opened her brown lunch bag and pulled out her cellophane-wrapped salami sandwich and a can of juice.

She could see Mark through the open door. He hung back shyly on the fringe of Danielle's group. Charlie hated the adoring way he was looking at Danielle.

Mark waited until most of Danielle's friends had gone inside to the lunchroom. Charlie noticed that he drew his mouth into a thin, nervous line as he walked up to Danielle. The pretty, dark-haired girl turned from her two remaining friends and listened to what he had to say, then she threw her head back haughtily. "I most certainly will not go to Harry's Ice Cream Heaven with you after school!" she said in a shrill voice so loud that even Charlie could hear it from inside the cafeteria.

"This *fifth-grader* wants to buy *me* an ice-cream sundae after school," Danielle turned and told her friends in the same loud, mocking voice. The girls rolled their eyes and giggled at Danielle's words.

Charlie saw Mark's face turn red with embarrassment. He looked around as if trying to find an escape. "Go away, Junior," said one of Danielle's friends. Mark turned stiffly and walked back up the stairs.

Danielle linked arms with her friends and they strolled into the cafeteria, still laughing about Mark. "The nerve of that kid to ask me out," Charlie heard Danielle say as they passed by her table. "He couldn't be more than eleven, and I'm almost twelve and a half. He should know enough to have some respect for his elders."

Danielle's remarks brought a whole new round of uproarious laughter from the two girls at her side. Poor Mark. Charlie felt so badly for him. She rewrapped her sandwich and put it back in her bag. Stuffing the bag into her purse, she got up from the table. With only the slightest limp, she hurried to the doorway. Once around the corner, Charlie dropped any effort to fake a limp and raced up the stairs.

When she reached the first landing she stopped and looked around. Mark seemed to have disappeared. A sound of shuffling feet from above made her turn and gaze up to the next flight of stairs. Mark was sitting on the steps, his head in his hands.

She climbed the stairs to him, remembering to limp slightly as she went. "You okay?" she asked.

"Oh, no," Mark groaned, shaking his head forlornly. "You saw what happened, too?"

Charlie settled down on the steps beside him. "Danielle can be pretty mean. Believe me, I know. I have to see her twice a week in ballet class."

"She looks so nice. I thought she'd *be* nice."

Charlie tried to remember if she'd ever witnessed Danielle doing anything nice. No, she hadn't. "I think Danielle has two sides, conceited and mean. That's all I've ever seen her be. Maybe she has a nice

side that she only shows at night, or when she stands in a closet or something. I've never seen it."

Charlie's remarks made Mark smile a little. "How many kids saw what happened, do you think?"

"Oh, hardly anybody," Charlie assured him. "The only reason I saw what happened was because I was sitting by the door. And normally I would have been talking to Lindsey and Emma, and I wouldn't even have noticed."

"How come you aren't with them today?"

Charlie explained that they were practicing their part in *Swan Lake*. "I can't be in it because of my foot," she told him.

"What a drag," he said sympathetically. "I bet you're a really good dancer, too."

"Why do you think that?"

"I don't know," he said, turning to look at her. "You just look like you would be. You're kind of twinkly."

"Twinkly?" Charlie asked, surprised. She'd never thought of herself as *twinkly*. "Is that good?"

"It's good, I guess," he answered. "I could picture you playing a fairy princess or something, hopping around the place on your toes."

Charlie laughed. "Could you picture me as a swan? That's what I'd be if I was in the show."

Mark studied her. "I don't know. You have kind of a long neck like a swan. Can you sound like a swan?"

"I'm not exactly sure what swans sound like. Are you?"

Mark thought. "There were swans in the pond near

the house we rented last summer. Mostly they were quiet, but sometimes they would go *honk-eek*! *Honk-eek!*"

"Are you sure?" Charlie said with a small giggle. "I was telling Emma and Lindsey that I thought they went, *honkhonkhonk,* real fast, like that."

"They do go kind of fast," he admitted. "Maybe it's *honk-eekhonk-eekhonk-eeeek!*"

At that moment, Mr. O'Neill turned the corner of the first landing and looked up at them. "What's all this honking I hear?" he asked sternly.

Charlie and Mark tried to look serious, but they were having trouble controlling their smiles. "I was just telling Mark about the show my ballet class is doing in the mall on Eastbridge Day. It has swans in it," Charlie explained.

"Yes, I recall the flyers," said Mr. O'Neill, sounding a little less official. "Why aren't you at lunch or in the playground? You know you're not supposed to be out here in the halls." The principal pulled his pink detention pad from inside his jacket pocket.

"Oh, no, please," Charlie begged. "I haven't gotten the nerve to tell my parents about the last detention slip you gave me. We were just talking."

A small smile made its way onto Mr. O'Neill's lips. "All right, but get down to the cafeteria and do your talking there from now on."

"Thanks," Mark said as he rose to his feet. He offered Charlie his hand to help her get up, and she took it. The quivery, jittery feeling came over her again, but this time it wasn't so scary. And there was another feeling along with it. A nice, warm feeling.

Mark wasn't just some cute boy who had this strange power over her. He was a person, just like she was. Someone who had crushes, disappointments, and embarrassing moments, just as she did.

"I'll help you," he said, taking her arm once again.

Somehow Charlie didn't want to lie to him anymore. She didn't want to lie to anyone. She suddenly felt foolish about having worried so much about what he would think if he saw her in the show. She had just seen other people laughing at him—and it didn't make her like him any less. Maybe it had made her like him even more.

"I think I can make it by myself," she said, leaning on the banister, just so her recovery wouldn't seem too abrupt. "My foot is really feeling better for some reason."

"That's great," he said as they walked down the stairs together. "Too bad you don't think it will be all better in time for the show."

Charlie frowned for a moment and then turned to him. "You know, I'm pretty sure I *will* be okay in time for the show," she said.

"You'd better hurry up and find out exactly what sound a swan makes, then," he kidded her.

"Please," she said in a faked tone of offense. "I am not going to be a regular swan. I am going to be a magical swan."

Chapter Eight

"Let me see the poor ankle, mademoiselle." Miss Claudine knelt down in front of Charlie, who sat on the dressing room bench.

Charlie held up her ankle. "It's really fine now," she assured her teacher.

"Yes, it looks just fine," Miss Claudine agreed with a smile. "And I am so happy you won't miss the performance. There is nothing like a real audience to spur you on to do your best work."

Charlie smiled weakly at Miss Claudine. "I hope I'll do okay," she said.

Miss Claudine patted Charlie's knee as she rose to her feet. "If you relax and concentrate on finding your center, you'll be fine," she said. "You have real spirit and shining eyes. You have what they call stage presence."

Charlie was delighted and a little surprised by Miss Claudine's words. Up until now, she'd thought that the only thing Miss Claudine had noticed about her was the fact that she was terrible at ballet. "Even if you don't perform the steps as perfectly as some others, the audience will still watch you," Miss Claudine continued, sitting beside her now on the bench. "It is one of the great mysteries of the performing arts. Some people have presence and others don't. And you have it."

"Thanks," Charlie said.

"I am just telling you what I see," Miss Claudine said, getting up and walking to the door. "Now hurry. The others are already being fitted for their costumes." Miss Claudine went out, leaving Charlie alone in the dressing room.

She thought about Miss Claudine's words as she pulled off her corduroy pants and stepped into her pink tights. Stage presence. No one had ever told her that before.

She walked over to the mirror on the dressing room wall and gazed into it, trying to see if her eyes were indeed shining as Miss Claudine had said. They just looked like plain old hazel eyes to her.

Charlie left the mirror and pulled on her leotard. She tied on her soft ballet shoes and then headed out to join the others.

The studio was in a chaotic state. The girls were not practicing at the barre, as usual. Instead they were in small groups, some practicing their steps, others just talking.

Danielle was the only one who was costumed. She did look pretty in a white leotard top and full white tulle skirt that fell to the middle of her thighs. She wore white tights and silky white toe shoes that were laced and crisscrossed around her ankles with satin ribbon. A boy with curly blond hair from her intermediate class stood with her. He was as tall as Danielle and would be playing the prince. Together the boy and Danielle went through the steps of the ballet.

Charlie looked around for Lindsey and Emma. Usually they all drove to class together in the car pool their parents had set up, but today Charlie's mother had driven her to the mall separately. She'd had to do some shopping anyway, so Charlie decided to surprise her friends by just showing up.

At first there was no sign of them, but then Emma's voice made Charlie turn. "Look who's here!" Emma shouted as she came into the studio, staggering under the weight of a big cardboard box.

"I decided I felt better, after all," Charlie said.

"That's great," cried Lindsey, who had followed Emma in, also carrying a box. Behind her came Adrian, his face hidden by the three boxes he carried.

And behind him was Marion Sweeney—Miss Claudine's former student, who was now a Radio City Music Hall Rockette. The girls knew her because she'd taken over a few of the classes last fall when Miss Claudine had been out sick. Charlie smiled at the sight of her. Marion Sweeney was a lot of fun.

"Hey, kid, I heard you hurt yourself," Marion Sweeney called, blowing a piece of her orange-red hair out of her eyes.

"I'm better now," Charlie answered. "What's in the boxes?"

"Costumes," the woman answered, kneeling and tearing open the taped seam of a box. "You kids are going to be the snazziest-looking swans anyone has ever seen."

At that moment, Miss Claudine came in holding an armful of white tulle. She dropped the tulle on the floor and put her hands on her hips. "What *is* all this, Marion?" she asked, laughter in her voice. "I asked you to see if you could pick up a few odds and ends in the city. I didn't mean for you to bring a truckload."

"No problem," Marion Sweeney assured her. "The costume lady at the Music Hall is a friend of mine. She knows she can trust me to bring it all back. Besides, no one's used this stuff since last year when we did a performance called *Birds of Paradise*. You should have seen it."

Marion Sweeney pulled something white and feathery out of the box. It was a white plastic headband with fake, downy white feathers trailing from it. She placed the feathery band onto her own head. "We were all kicking in formation while we were dressed as birds. Every night there were feathers all over the stage."

Miss Claudine smiled happily as she knelt and ran her hands through the soft contents of the opened box. Bunches of airy fake feathers were held together with rubber bands and safety pins. The feathers were white, pastel pink, and baby blue.

Miss Claudine turned to Adrian. "*Mon chéri,* would you start running the girls through the steps?" Adrian was a dancer, too, and sometimes he helped teach Miss Claudine's classes.

As Emma, Lindsey, and the rest of the class went

into their groups, Charlie looked at Miss Claudine in distress. "Where should I stand?" she asked.

"You will be my model for now," Miss Claudine answered.

"Don't you think I ought to practice?" Charlie objected.

Miss Claudine smoothed her hair and seemed to study Charlie for a moment. "No," she said. "I will show you the steps later. Trying to pick them up now would just discourage you. Step into one of those tutus on the floor."

Charlie reached into the pile and pulled out a short, round clump of tulle. She stretched the elastic band which held the material together and stepped into it, pulling it to her waist.

Miss Claudine took a handful of feathers from the box. Carefully, she pinned one bunch to each shoulder of Charlie's leotard. She leaned back on her heels to study the effect. "Hmmm," she mused thoughtfully. Then, as if inspired, Miss Claudine began arranging the feathers—some in Charlie's hair, some at her wrists and ankles. "*Voilà!*" she said at last.

"Not bad at all," said Marion Sweeney, who had been watching from the doorway.

Charlie looked in the big mirror behind her. She hardly recognized herself, but she liked what she saw. She had been transformed into a strange, magical creature, half-girl, half-bird. She lifted her arms and flapped her hands as if they were wings.

"That's it!" laughed Miss Claudine. "It is wonderful how a costume transforms one."

Miss Claudine signaled for Adrian to stop the class.

She presented Charlie and instructed them on how they could go about creating a similar costume for themselves. "Gather the pieces you need from the boxes and help one another. Keep to this general idea, but the feathers need not be pinned in exactly the same way. I want each of you to express your own inner swan."

Soon the room was a flurry of feathers as the girls experimented with different ways to attach them. Charlie helped Emma and Lindsey put together their costumes.

Emma plunged right in, weaving ribbons full of feathers through her long dark hair until feathers stuck out at all angles. "I think you've gone a little overboard, don't you?" Lindsey criticized, looking skeptically at Emma's feathery hairdo.

Examining the effect in the mirror, Emma shrugged. "I kind of like it, but maybe you're right. It wouldn't really go with what everyone else is doing."

"I can't believe you care what everyone else is doing," said Charlie, who expected Emma to insist on being totally unique.

"We're the corps de ballet," Emma told her seriously. "We're not supposed to distract the audience from watching the principal dancer."

Charlie looked at Emma in amazement. "You mean you actually want them to pay attention to Danielle?"

"It's not for Danielle's sake," explained Lindsey, experimenting with different ways to position her feathered headband. "It's for Miss Claudine, so the show will look good. Face it, even though she's a snot, Danielle's a better dancer than any of us. It would be better for Miss Claudine if the audience looks at Danielle and not at us."

Charlie was astonished. Normally she'd have expected Emma and Lindsey to be plotting ways to make Danielle look bad—and giggling all through it. But they were very serious about wanting this show to be successful.

"I look so dumb in this tutu thing," Lindsey grumbled. She continued to mutter as she adjusted the tulle skirt at her waist. Yet she was wearing it. Charlie remembered a time when Lindsey wouldn't even wear her leotard without a T-shirt over it.

Miss Claudine took Charlie aside and ran through the ballet steps with her. Most of them Charlie already knew, since they'd begun practicing before she hurt her ankle. But her time away from class had made her even worse than before. Her feet seemed incapable of doing anything other than tripping each other.

"I'm really trying, Miss Claudine," Charlie told her teacher. "I thought the costume would help, but I guess not."

"You will get performance energy," Miss Claudine said, though her voice had a doubtful tone to it. "Remember: relax and concentrate."

Charlie wasn't sure she could do both at once. It seemed to her that you either relaxed *or* you concentrated. She looked once again at her reflection in the mirror. The costume didn't look so wonderful now.

What right did she have to wear it when she couldn't even get the steps right?

Miss Claudine positioned Charlie in the back of a double line of girls. The rehearsal did *not* go well. Even though Charlie tumbled over her own two feet more than the others, all the girls were making mistakes. They bumped into one another and did different steps at different times.

The boy, named Stephen Graves, was very good as the Prince. He danced his part confidently, but Danielle was all nerves. She missed steps she'd done well all along.

Miss Claudine slumped against the barre as she watched the dress rehearsal. Marion Sweeney patted her shoulder. When the music stopped, Miss Claudine checked her watch. "It's late, but let's try it one more time," she said gloomily. "Remember that the performance is only three days away."

Chapter Nine

"Okay, now here's where Danielle starts spinning to the ground and we gather around her," said Emma as she stood in arabesque position in Charlie's living room. Lindsey and Charlie followed Emma as she fluttered in a circle and then stopped by the imaginary Swan Princess with her hands crossed in front of her.

"Lovely!" Mrs. Clark applauded from the doorway between the kitchen and the living room.

"We're slightly less terrible than we were, anyway," said Lindsey, plopping down on the couch.

"I can't practice anymore," Emma said, joining Lindsey on the couch. "I'm pooped."

"I think I kind of know where I'm supposed to be," said Charlie, throwing herself down next to Lindsey. "Thanks for going through it with me. It's a lot to remember, though."

Mrs. Clark looked at the three girls sprawled dismally against one another and laughed. "What a sad sight!"

"You don't understand, Mom," said Charlie. "Everyone's going to be looking at us on Saturday, and we're terrible!"

"And if the show doesn't go well, no one will sign up for dance lessons, and the school might close down," Emma added.

"You girls are being too hard on yourselves," said Mrs. Clark. "Everyone knows this is a beginners' class. Would some homemade chocolate-chip cookies cheer you up?"

"No, thanks," said Emma, dragging herself to her feet. "I think I'll just go home and rest."

"Me, too," Lindsey said, joining Emma. "Thanks anyway."

Charlie didn't bother to show her friends out, but stayed slumped on the couch. "Bye," she said with a wave. They flapped their hands back at her and headed out the door.

Mrs. Clark sat down next to Charlie. "I'm very proud of you, you know," she said.

"What for?" asked Charlie, truly bewildered.

"I know you didn't want to be in this show. And your ankle would have given you a perfect excuse to stay out of it."

Charlie looked at her mother. "Mom, I have to tell you something," she began. Swallowing, she continued, "My ankle was better before I told you it was."

Mrs. Clark smiled softly. "I know."

"You knew!"

"I spoke with Dr. Janklow about your ankle, and she asked me if there was something coming up that you didn't want to do. That's when I realized it was the show. Besides, you're a very bad limper. Sometimes you'd limp to the left, and other times to the right. And then sometimes you'd drag your foot behind. There were times when you'd simply forget to limp altogether. Most people limp one way or another, not ten different ways."

Despite her embarrassment, Charlie smiled. "I didn't want to lie to you. I just couldn't face being in that show."

"What made you change your mind?" asked her mother.

Charlie sighed. "I don't know. Miss Claudine's been really nice to me and it didn't feel right letting her down. And then—you know that boy I was telling you about? Mark?" Her mother nodded. "Well, I was worried because he's coming to the show, but I got talking to him, and he didn't seem like the kind of person who'd laugh if I made a mistake."

"He must be nice."

"He is," Charlie agreed.

Mrs. Clark put her arm around Charlie. "The reason I'm proud of you is because you're doing something hard, and you're doing it to help someone else."

"You won't be so proud when you see the show."

"It doesn't matter," said her mother. "Lots of people never challenge themselves to do things they find hard. They never grow."

Charlie let her mother's words sink in. The word "grow" stuck in her head. It seemed to Charlie that growing up was confusing. Part of her couldn't wait to be big, but another part wanted to stay a little girl forever, so she wouldn't have to do hard things like be in this show. "Is it hard to be a grown-up?" she asked her mother.

Mrs. Clark thought about the question. "In some ways it's harder than being a kid, and in other ways it's easier. I think it has to do with making decisions. It's great making your own decisions, but it can be scary, too."

"You know what? I liked being babied when my ankle hurt," Charlie admitted. "I liked it so much, it was one of the reasons I didn't say anything about feeling better."

Mrs. Clark squeezed her daughter. "We all need to be babied sometimes. You'll always be *my* baby, no matter how big you get."

Charlie smiled and wrapped her arms around her mother's waist. She felt happy and safe sitting next to her like that. Maybe growing up wouldn't be so bad if she just took it slowly.

Still, she hadn't stopped worrying altogether. It was hard standing up in front of a lot of strangers. And harder still when you were sure they were going to be laughing at you. She wished she could just sit like this on the couch, safe in her mother's arms forever. Or at least until after Eastbridge Day.

At that moment Harry and John came bursting in the front door, their clothes caked with mud from a neighborhood game of football. "Go straight upstairs and wash," Mrs. Clark ordered. "Don't even sit down or touch anything until you're clean and out of those clothes."

The boys headed up the stairs, but John stopped

midway. "Hey, squirt, me and my friends are all coming to see you on Saturday."

"It's really okay, you don't have to," Charlie assured him.

"We're *really* going to see Pip Douglass who's signing footballs for Eastbridge Day over at John's Sports. We'll be in the mall, anyway."

"You guys better not yell or whistle or anything," Charlie warned her brother.

John put his hand to his chest daintily and pretended to be deeply hurt. "I can't believe you would think such a thing of me and my friends. Is it all right with you if we just shoot spitballs at that Danielle girl?"

Charlie giggled at the thought. "No, it wouldn't be all right," she told him. "Wait until *after* the performance."

"You two are *bad,*" said Mrs. Clark. "Now scoot. Don't you both have homework you should be doing?" John ran back up the stairs, and Mrs. Clark returned to the kitchen, leaving Charlie alone in the living room.

Charlie went to her bedroom and began her homework, but she couldn't concentrate on it. All she could think about was the show. Or Mark Johnson. Or Mark Johnson watching the show.

Would he be as nice when he was with all his friends? She wished she could stop thinking about him and worrying.

She spent the next two days in a series of up and down moods. She wasn't sure if she wanted Saturday to come and go, or if she wished it would never arrive

77

at all. She could tell Emma and Lindsey were tense, too. Once Emma even came to school with no makeup on. Charlie decided that was a bad sign.

On Saturday morning, Charlie's eyes snapped open. The sun was just coming up. She tried to go back to sleep, but she couldn't. She lay awake and stared at the ceiling until her mother knocked on her bedroom door at about eight. "Get up. We have to be at Miss Claudine's in an hour," she called.

Charlie suddenly sat bolt upright in her bed. "I can't," she whimpered, feeling something in her stomach lunge forward. "I'm going to be sick."

Chapter Ten

"It was just a bad case of butterflies," said Mrs. Clark as she turned the car into the parking lot of the Eastbridge Mall. It didn't feel like anything as friendly as butterflies to Charlie. It felt like being plain old sick to her stomach.

"I felt kind of sick today, too," said Lindsey.

"My throat feels dry," added Emma.

"We'll be okay—I hope," Charlie told them bravely.

Mrs. Clark parked the car at the back entrance to the mall. "Good luck," she said, leaning over to kiss Charlie on the cheek. "Look for us in the audience."

"Thanks," said Charlie, sliding out of her seat.

She walked with Emma and Lindsey through the mall to Miss Claudine's. "Just don't think about it," Emma advised. "Pretend it's just another ballet class. That's what I'm doing."

The girls entered the school and saw that the studio was a whirlwind of activity. Students from all of

Miss Claudine's classes were bustling about noisily. Marion Sweeney was helping the beginners to pin feathers and adjust tutus. All the girls were fussing with their hair and costumes. Miss Claudine sat at a small card table applying makeup to the girls who were already dressed.

Charlie, Lindsey, and Emma joined their class. Stephen Graves was there, dressed in his costume: green tights, a brown tunic, and a brown huntsman's cap. He carried a case of plastic arrows over his shoulder and a plastic toy bow in his hands.

"He looks cute," said Emma, gazing at the blond boy.

"And he's going to shoot Danielle," added Lindsey. "Even if it's just pretend, that's okay by me."

The girls got into their leotards and tights and joined the others in the studio. "Come on, kids, let's get you feathered up," called Marion Sweeney.

Emma, Lindsey, and Charlie reached into the open boxes of feathers and feathered headbands and began putting their costumes together. Charlie looked over at Miss Claudine and noticed how serious her expression was as she applied thick black liner to a student's eyes—and she remembered how important this performance was to her teacher.

"Has anyone seen Danielle?" asked Miss Claudine.

Marion Sweeney looked around the room. "She was here a second ago. Charlie, would you peek into the dressing room and see if she's there?"

"Okay," Charlie replied. She wrinkled up her nose at Emma and Lindsey to show that she didn't exactly adore the idea of looking for Danielle, and then she headed off for the dressing room.

Charlie found Danielle sitting by herself on the edge of a bench. "Miss Claudine's looking for you," she said.

Danielle gazed at her with a blank expression and shook her head. "I can't go out there," she muttered. "I just can't."

Charlie was shocked. Could Danielle Sainte-Marie be scared to perform? Danielle, who was always so super-confident?

"You're just nervous," said Charlie. "So am I. Come on." Danielle didn't budge, so Charlie took hold of her wrist and gently pulled her to her feet. "Come *on*."

Danielle seemed to be in a dream world as she followed Charlie back out to the studio. Charlie directed her toward Miss Claudine and then rejoined Emma and Lindsey. "Boy, I thought *I* was nervous," she said to her friends. "Danielle is scared stiff!"

Emma raised her eyebrows. "She'd better not mess up. She's the star." Lindsey and Charlie nodded.

By ten-thirty, the class was costumed. "Now *chéries,*" said Miss Claudine, gathering all the girls around her. "The moment of performance is upon us. I will leave you with but one thought: find your centers. Breathe deeply and concentrate on that spot, low in your belly, where you are balanced and quiet. You know the steps and have practiced hard. When you are centered, your body will do the rest."

Charlie breathed, but there was no spot in her body that was balanced and quiet. Her stomach gurgled nervously and her heart was thumping. She looked at herself in the mirror. Every feather was in place, but somehow the magic hadn't set in. She just looked like plain old Charlie in a crazy bird suit.

"Come on," Lindsey called to her. "We're going." The classes were filing out behind Miss Claudine. Charlie ran and joined the others as they walked out the front door.

The mall was abuzz with excitement. Booths and tables were set up for the different stores to display their wares and services. A woman dressed as a gypsy sat in front of the New Age Mystical Book Shop and read palms. At Arthur's Video Palace shoppers were having their pictures taken with a life-size cutout of Frankenstein. An artist was drawing pictures of people in front of House of Frames. It was like a giant carnival.

Miss Claudine led them to the rectangular pool at the center of the mall. A flat wooden platform, which was to be the stage, had been set up beside the reflecting pool. Plastic potted plants were scattered around the sides of the platform.

"I get it," said Emma. "The pool is our lake."

"Neat," Lindsey said.

Rows of folding chairs had been set up at the edge of the pool, facing the platform. A large sign read: See Miss Claudine's School of Ballet Perform Scenes from *Swan Lake, The Nutcracker Suite,* and *Giselle.* Performances Begin at Twelve O'Clock. Registration for the New Session of Classes Immediately Afterward.

The classes clustered at the edge of the stage, the

beginners standing apart from the more advanced classes, waiting their turn. They watched anxiously as the audience arrived. By eleven, almost all the chairs were filled. Charlie could see Mr. and Mrs. Sainte-Marie sitting in the front row. She saw her own mother and father sitting in the center. Toward the back Emma's mother sat with Lindsey's father. Charlie's brother John was standing in the back with a group of his friends.

Terror filled her as she heard Miss Claudine playing the overture to *Swan Lake* on the new tape deck she'd bought just for the occasion. Danielle stood in front of her. The girl was pale as a ghost.

When they heard the music which was Danielle's cue to run to the center of the stage, Danielle didn't move. "Go!" Emma whispered, giving the girl a shove.

The shove did the trick, and Danielle ran gracefully toward the pool. Seconds later, the beginners were to follow her. The first girl began running. In that second Charlie caught sight of Mark Johnson and some boys from her class sitting in the audience.

Charlie saw the other girls going ahead of her—but her feet were frozen to the spot. She couldn't move. "Come on," whispered Lindsey. "We have to go." Still Charlie was unable to take a step. "Come on!" Lindsey urged again, yanking Charlie by the arm.

"Okay," Charlie whispered, breathless with anxiety. She forced her foot to step forward, and with that first step, the rest of her seemed to come alive. Before she knew it, she was following the others onto the platform.

Danielle danced stiffly, unable to shake her nervousness, but Stephen confidently steered her through the steps, covering up for her when she forgot her part. The rest of the class fluttered around her.

At one point, Charlie thought she was supposed to turn right. She turned and ran, toes pointed, to the far right of the stage—as the rest of the class went left! Charlie looked back over her shoulder. Where was everyone?

The audience laughed lightly when they realized what had happened. When Charlie heard the sound, she closed her eyes and made a wish. She wished to disappear off the planet forever. When she opened them, she looked down at the smiling faces in the audience. The faces were friendly, not mean, and Charlie realized nothing really terrible had happened. She smiled at the audience, flapped her arms, and scurried back over to the group.

Now the thing she was most worried about had happened—everyone had laughed at her. She'd made a big mistake in front of Mark Johnson. And it hadn't been such a disaster, after all.

She looked out at the audience and suddenly she felt a spot deep inside her that wasn't nervous—that was balanced and quiet. She raised her chin high and continued to dance, but now with new confidence. She suddenly trusted her feet to remember the steps. And they did.

For the first time since she'd begun classes, Charlie really enjoyed dancing. She felt the music carry her along. In her mind she was a magical swan.

At the end of the act Danielle fluttered to the

ground. Along with the other magical swans, Charlie gazed down at her sorrowfully.

Suddenly Charlie noticed that Danielle's back was moving up and down. She recognized the symptom from her morning of almost being ill. Danielle's nerves seemed to have gotten the best of her at last, and Charlie was afraid Danielle was about to be sick right there on the stage!

Charlie knew she couldn't let the audience see that. As much as she disliked Danielle, she didn't want Miss Claudine's performance ruined. She had to do something—and fast. But what?

There wasn't time to stand there and think about it. She had to move. "Follow me," she whispered to Lindsey, who stood in front of her. Charlie threw back her head and began to honk sadly—*honkhonkhonk*—leaping to the front of the chorus. The other girls had noticed what was happening, and followed as Charlie led them, skipping in a circle, until they formed a tight group in front of Danielle.

Never realizing that the Swan Princess was in any distress, the audience applauded. Slowly Danielle got to her feet and took a wobbly bow. Then she slapped her hand to her mouth and ran off the stage.

"The Swan Princess looks more like the 'Dying Duck' to me," whispered Emma. Charlie's lips twitched into a smile, but she held her pose as the audience continued to clap.

Charlie was thrilled by the sound of the applause. She let it wash over her. Out of the corner of her eye she noticed that even the advanced classes were clapping loudly for them. From out in the audience, she

heard shrill whistling and a familiar voice yelling, "All right, Charlie! Way to go!" She knew it was her brother John shouting. She felt the heat of a blush creeping up her neck. She wasn't upset, though. The smile on her face just grew broader.

Then, as Miss Claudine had instructed them, the girls fluttered away from the pond and off the stage. Miss Claudine was waiting for them. "I am so proud, proud of you all!" she said happily. She threw her arms wide and hugged each of them.

When she got to Charlie, Miss Claudine hugged her and then kissed her quickly on the forehead. "You were *très magnifique,*" she whispered. "A quick mind and star quality—a winning combination," she added, patting Charlie on the back lightly.

Just then, a woman interrupted Miss Claudine. "Your girls seemed to be having such fun," the woman said. "I'd like to sign my Emily up for classes."

Another woman came up behind the first one. "I think my daughter would really benefit from this experience," she said. Before long, Miss Claudine was surrounded by parents wanting to sign their children up for classes. She smiled at them all. "Ballet trains the body and the mind," Charlie heard Miss Claudine tell the parents. "Please, won't you stay to see my other classes perform?"

Charlie looked around and saw that Emma and Lindsey were beside the stage talking to their parents. Charlie headed toward her own parents and suddenly stopped short. Mark Johnson was coming her way.

She didn't know what to do. Should she pretend

she didn't see him? Or stand and wait for him to reach her? Maybe he wasn't coming to talk to *her* at all. Charlie stood where she was and pretended to be fixing a feather in her costume.

Mark stopped in front of her shyly, his hands behind his back. Charlie looked up and pretended to be surprised to see him. "Oh, hi, Mark," she said as naturally as she could.

"You were really good," he said.

"Thanks."

He pulled a bouquet of chrysanthemums from behind his back. "Congratulations."

Charlie took the flowers. "Where did you—" she started to ask, and then remembered the pots of the same fluffy white flowers scattered in barrels around the mall in honor of Eastbridge Day. "You're not supposed to pick these," she whispered with a grin. Mark shrugged, a mischievous twinkle in his eye.

"Hey, Johnson!" a boy called. "Are you coming, or what?"

"Hang on, I'll be right there," Mark shouted to his friend. He turned back to Charlie. "I've got to go. See you in school."

"Yeah, see you," said Charlie happily. "And thanks for the flowers."

"No problem." She watched him hurry away, then he stopped and turned. "Oh, and I think you got the honk just right," he called.

Charlie laughed. "Thanks."

Still sniffing her bouquet, Charlie found her parents. "You were the best one in the whole show," her father told her. Charlie knew it wasn't the truth, but it was nice to hear.

"You did a wonderful job," her mother agreed. "I thought you were just wonderful . . . just wonderful." Charlie saw tears glistening in her mother's eyes.

"Are you okay, Mom?" she asked.

Charlie's father laughed and handed her mother a tissue. "Didn't you know your mother always cries when she's happy? She sobbed all through our wedding ceremony."

"Frank, you exaggerate," said Mrs. Clark, wiping her eyes. "But I *am* very proud of you, Charlie. You were terrific."

"Thanks, Mom." Charlie's face was starting to hurt from smiling. The day she'd dreaded was turning out to be one of the best days of her life.

Emma and Lindsey came over, and Charlie handed them each a flower from her bouquet. "We did it," said Emma.

"And we're still alive," added Lindsey.

"We sure are," Charlie agreed, still smiling. "We sure are."

Emma Guthrie, Charlie Clark, and Lindsey Munson aren't exactly thrilled about taking ballet lessons. But things get even worse when Emma decides to dance her way into the limelight—on her toes! Don't miss her hilarious debut in *Pointing Toward Trouble,* book #5 in the NO WAY BALLET series.